Angel's Journey

A Bullied Filly's Search for Friends & Purpose

Illustration by
Rachel Tryba

Digital Artistry by
Courtney Vail

Authorship by
Courtney Vail & Sandra J. Howell

A WEST RIDGE FARM PUBLISHING PRODUCTION
westridgefarmpublishing.com

Staring at the colorful sky, I sniffed the air for sweet clover. I know I smelled it. This farm has the best food. Pink Lady owns it. She gives me apples, carrots and mints for treats, but I love clover the most.

I looked all over the ground.

Aha! Found it!

I bent to gobble up a bud with a cluster of yummy greens, then jerked back at a hop. "Oh! Mister Frog. You spooked me," I said, lifting my head. "I didn't see you there."

He hopped to the pond outside my fence. "You are odd, Little Filly," Mister Frog said by the water. "Why are you not with the other horses? You're always off by yourself."

"They bully me for being so curly and not sleek like them. I also like to think and dream. They only run and play. As much as I like to leap in the rain or wait for a butterfly to land on my nose, I want to do something big and amazing. I want to be a big hero and not a nothing...a nobody...just a big zero."

"Silly girl. You lack good sense too," he said. "You are a horse. Of course, you will grow very big."

I hoofed the ground and puffed through my nose. "That's not what I meant. Not big in size. Big in importance."

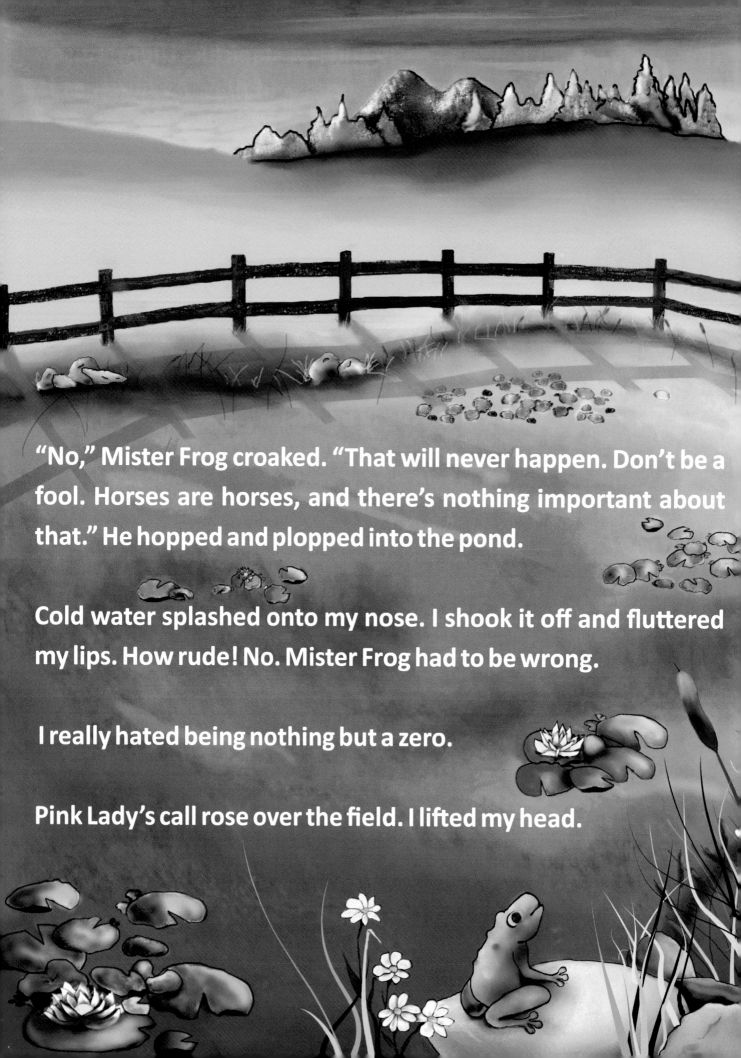

"No," Mister Frog croaked. "That will never happen. Don't be a fool. Horses are horses, and there's nothing important about that." He hopped and plopped into the pond.

Cold water splashed onto my nose. I shook it off and fluttered my lips. How rude! No. Mister Frog had to be wrong.

I really hated being nothing but a zero.

Pink Lady's call rose over the field. I lifted my head.

Cookie time!

Uh-oh. I looked this way and that. Did I walk too far out again? Where am I? And where is the barn? If I walk away from the low sun, I should find it.

And I did! Woo-hoo. I could see it up ahead. I won.

When I got to the barn, New Man said, "I love your white coat and pretty curls. You'd make the perfect circus horse."

Circus? Yes. Stars filled my eyes. I could just see myself trotting out under the lights. Maybe the horses there will like me and I will have friends at last.

I was happy to get into his trailer for a new life. The ride was long, and I fell asleep. When we finally came to a stop, I woke up to a new place with new smells and sounds.

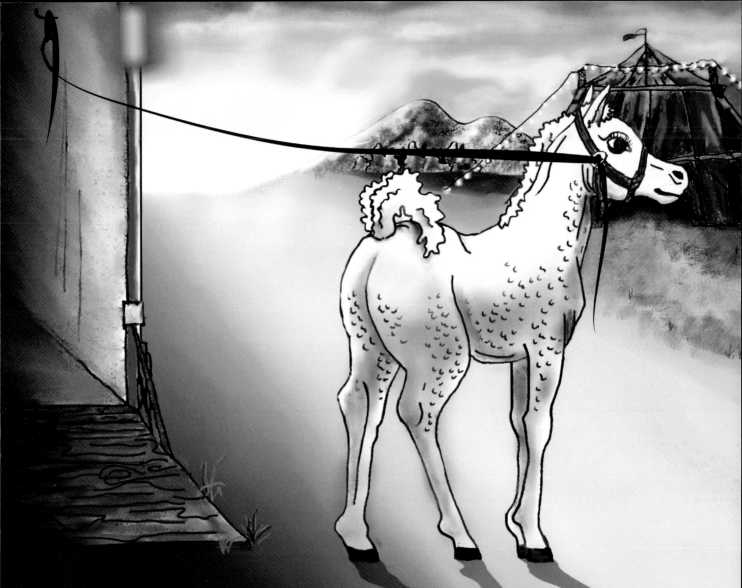

My heart raced. I was scared to be off the farm but ready for my time to shine. How can you be a hero if you don't get chances to be brave? I had to be brave. I will be brave. I will not be a zero here.

New Man led me out. "Welcome to the circus, Miss Curly."

Buttered popcorn, colorful balloons, joyful music and the cheering crowd all seemed fun.

Yes! Bet I can be a hero here.

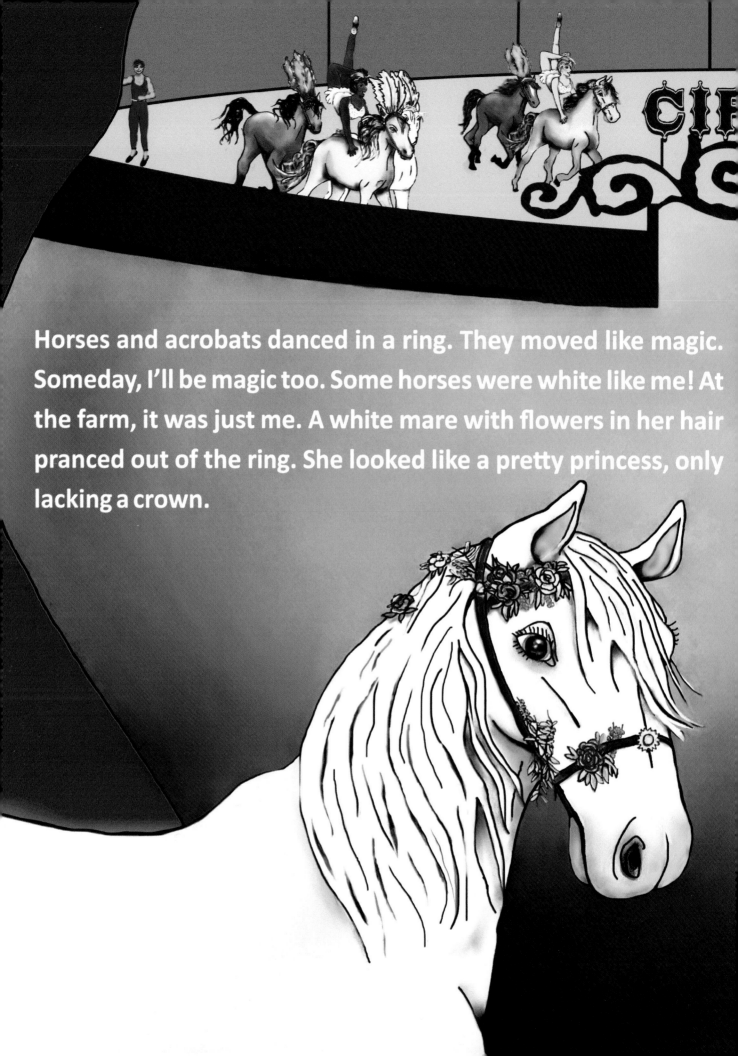

Horses and acrobats danced in a ring. They moved like magic. Someday, I'll be magic too. Some horses were white like me! At the farm, it was just me. A white mare with flowers in her hair pranced out of the ring. She looked like a pretty princess, only lacking a crown.

Princess saw me standing there. "Uh! Why are your mane and tail so curly, Frizz Ball? Awful! Did you get left out in the rain?"

I shook my head. "No. My hair is just like this."

"Well, I have never seen a mess like that. Your coat is wild too. It'll take days for it to look tidy."

I looked down and scraped the ground with my hoof. Yuck. Maybe I really am ugly like the farm horses said.

After getting a horse cookie, she was led away. Great. Would all the horses hate me here too?

Wait! Hope bloomed in my heart when I saw a big, black horse out there. He marched like a king. His mane and tail were wavy too! I wasn't the only one with curls. The crowd cheered for him the most as he clip-clopped out of the tent.

Seeing me, King stopped. "Whoa. Who are you, Little Girl?"

"I am nothing really, a nobody. But...I *will be* a hero like you someday. And a big star. You made all the kids clap and smile."

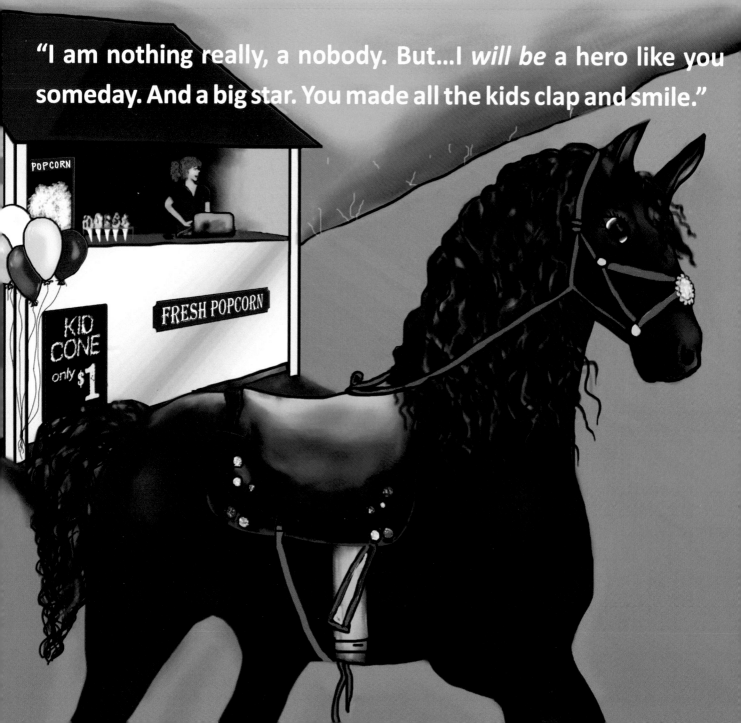

"They only clap and smile for the tricks, Sweetie. That's not heroic. It's just…life," King said.

No. He was wrong. He had to be. I mean, they cheered and even tossed flowers into the ring. I shook my head as King left. My dream of being important began to crumble.

I really, really hated being nothing but a zero.

Within two years, I learned all the tricks. I bowed and leaped, danced a little to the left, and a little to the right. Acrobats flipped on and off my back and wove around me as I ran in circles. I also did my own move, dropping to the ground for young performers to mount, then standing and taking a bow. I got lots of kisses from the dogs and treats from the kids.

But...King had been right, and I still had no friends.

Even as a big star, I was still a big zero.

"How do I become a hero?" I said in my lonely stall to no one.

"Don't take my popcorn. That is one way," a mouse replied, stunning me as he stopped in his scurry across my gate.

"Not to worry, Mouse. I don't even like popcorn. I am a big star now. So, why am I still a big, bullied nobody?"

Not a beast of many words, Mouse simply said, "Squeak louder," before darting off.

Okay. I tried that. I talked a lot more to the other horses. But they were still mean to me. They were still big bullies.

One day, I jumped for joy when I heard King tell Princess, "She has grown into a fine mare."

"No," Princess said with a flutter of her lips. "Not really. She's too small, nothing but a shrimp, and all those curls are ugly. She will never, ever dazzle. She needs to go."

Why did everyone hate me? The circus agreed with Princess and my star days were over.

I was sold to White Beard. He did not care that I was too short or curly. I was glad to be back on a farm again.

He loved to show me off in town parades and have kids come visit to groom me and give me yummy treats.

Life was fun. But...I still wasn't doing anything great.

I was still a big zero.

"I love it on this farm, Buzz," I said on one bright night to the cat who shared my barn. "But...how do I live with purpose? I really want to be a hero." I did not know I had yanked Buzz out of a deep sleep on the beam above me until an acorn bopped me on the head. "Ow." I ducked, fearing he'd swat more at me.

Good with the one, Buzz jumped down to the floor. "By loving every nap and sunrise of course." He stretched his back. "Naps are very purrrrposeful."

I flapped my lips. Sure, fine for a cat, but what about me?

I worked to be perfect for White Beard, and he loved me a lot, but he got sick one day and had to leave home. I ate up all the hay and grass in my fence. Many days passed, and I got hungry and cold in just the run-in shed. My coat, once fluffy like clouds, became smelly, muddy, and gross. Even Buzz took off.

Just in time, a man in a cap showed up and saved me. I was loaded on a trailer next to a perfect, black horse.

What a showoff too!

Showoff shined like marble and his mane hung long and sleek.

Chatty Girl had come with Cap Man and could not stop talking about his good looks.

We were driven to their big farm and backed out of the trailer into clean, fresh air. Green hills rolled on and on.

I took a whiff and could already smell the sweet hay and clover. More horses than I could count stood out grazing. I did not know if I would ever be a hero here, but I was happy to be safe in a land with so much to eat.

Showoff sniffed the air too. "It's a new start for us," he said with a showy flick and whirl of his tail.

"Yep." Knowing I'd never look *that* perfect, I hung my head low, and even lower, when two girls rushed over, one on wheels.

The girl who rolled over in a wheelchair had curly, red hair. I liked her a lot, but Red looked afraid of me. To show her I was nice, I kissed her cheek. That made her giggle.

Chatty Girl's other friend with dark hair could not stop smiling at me. Raven loved me right away. I think she could even see a hero under this mess. The twinkle in her eyes said so.

Chatty Girl led me to a fence. "Uh, she's such a disaster."

"Aw, don't say that," Raven said. "She just needs some love and good feed...and a bath."

"Hmm. More like five," Chatty Girl said.

"Give her a break." Raven opened the gate. "Even with the hard road she's been on, she is still so sweet. I love her already."

"Yeah, she kissed me," Red said, daring to reach up and scratch my muddy head again.

I bopped her arm to show her we were friends now.

"She'd make the perfect therapy horse," Raven said.

Therapy? My ears twitched.

"She would," Red said. "To help kids like me. She's an Angel. In fact, let's call her that."

Angel? Yes! Perfect.

That name held purpose. That was so me. I nodded.

They giggled and led me to a safe spot with fresh hay and a tub of cool water. I loved having food again…and true friends for the first time ever.

Three mares in the field next to me were glaring at me.

"Eww. She's so gross," I heard one say.

"I know. She looks nothing like us. This is a therapy farm. We have important work to do."

"Hey! Mud Monster," one cried. "You a freak or something?"

More bullies? Great. I kept my nose in the hay pile.

I really, really, really hated being nothing but a zero.

After weeks of good feed, grooming, training and love from Raven, Red, and even Chatty Girl, I grew good and strong.

I showed them my old circus tricks and learned all their new cues. I wanted to win this time. I had to. I hoped to work in therapy to help kids like Red.

My hard work paid off, and I won a spot.

As I was led into the arena for the first time, a reddish brown mare said, "Welcome to the Big Top, Angel. You made it. Today is your day to shine." Ginger's brown eyes looked warmly at me, and I knew I had found my first horse friend.

"I think so." I could feel it in my bones. I looked around, taking it all in. There were no clowns, balloons, or dancing dogs. There was no pizzazz to hide behind. It was all up to me.

When a lady helped a small, happy girl with leg braces over to me, I dropped to the ground to show off my talent.

"*What*...are you doing?" Ginger muttered in shock.

"Don't worry. This is one of my very own circus tricks." But I got butterflies in my belly when people gasped.

Uh oh. Did I make a wrong move?

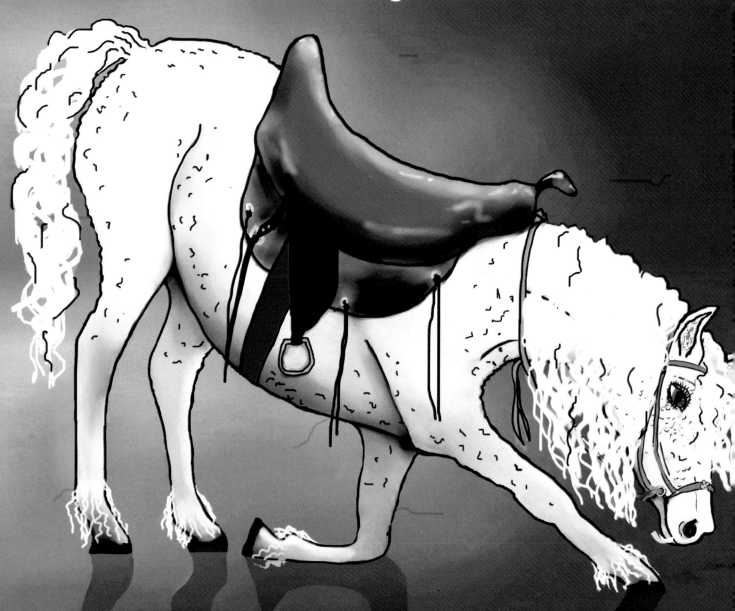

After Happy was sitting steady on my saddle, she took the reins and inched her feet into the stirrups. Our helper stayed beside us, but I knew I could rock this. As I stood, everyone cheered.

Ha! Take that, all you mean bullies!

"Whoa, cool." Happy fluttered her fingers between my ears. "Hi, Angel. None of the other horses here can do that. You're amazing. I've never seen a curly horse before either. You're so pretty and fluffy and special. I can't walk that good...*yet*. So, thanks for being my legs today. Thanks...for being my hero."

Yes. Finally! A hero at last.

My time, my moment had come.

At Happy's soft tap on my side, I nodded and walked on.

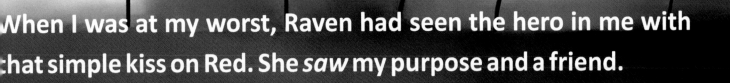

When I was at my worst, Raven had seen the hero in me with that simple kiss on Red. She *saw* my purpose and a friend.

I now believe, if *I* can make the world brighter with one kind act, then *anyone* can.

And there's absolutely nothing "Zero" about that!

Follow more of Angel's adventures,
as well as those of her human friends,
in the award-winning Angels Club Series.

Appropriate, exciting and fun for all ages.

angelsclubkids.com